Good-bye, Sheepie

BY

ROBERT BURLEIGH

ILLUSTRATED BY

PETER CATALANOTTO

MARSHALL CAVENDISH CHILDREN

Text copyright © 2010 by Robert Burleigh
Illustrations copyright © 2010 by Peter Catalanotto
Marshall Cavendish Corporation
99 White Plains Road
Tarrytown, NY 10591
www.marshallcavendish.us/kids

Library of Congress Cataloging-in-Publication Data

Burleigh, Robert.
  Good-bye, Sheepie / by Robert Burleigh ;
illustrated by Peter Catalanotto.–1st ed.
    p. cm.
  Summary: A father teaches his young son about death
and remembering as he buries their beloved dog.
  ISBN 978-0-7614-5598-1
  [1. Death–Fiction. 2. Dogs–Fiction. 3. Fathers and sons–
Fiction.] I. Catalanotto, Peter, ill. II. Title.
  PZ7.B9244Goo 2010
  [E]–dc22   2009005955

The illustrations are rendered in watercolor and gouache.
Book design by Vera Soki
Editor: Margery Cuyler

Printed in Malaysia (T)
First edition
1 3 5 6 4 2

mc **Marshall Cavendish**
Children

To my children: in memory of our farmhouse days
—R.B.

To King, Gemini, Beau, Cha Cha, Mary Jane, and Painter
A special thanks to Sarah and E-Boy
—P.C.

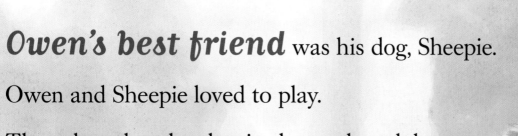

Owen's best friend was his dog, Sheepie.

Owen and Sheepie loved to play.

They chased each other in the yard, took long walks, and even slept together at night.

But Sheepie was getting old.

When Owen threw a stick, Sheepie would stand and look sadly at his friend. Then he would limp out to find the stick in the tall grass.

Sometimes Owen had to help him climb the stairs. And Sheepie was sleeping more and more.

One afternoon, Owen walked outside and found
Sheepie lying under the big oak tree. Owen patted
him, but Sheepie didn't lift his head or wag his tail.

He just lay very still.

Owen ran and got his father. Owen's dad took
hold of his hand.

They stood quietly, looking at Sheepie.
Dad spoke softly. "Poor Sheepie. He was hurting.
We knew he couldn't live forever."

Owen began to cry.

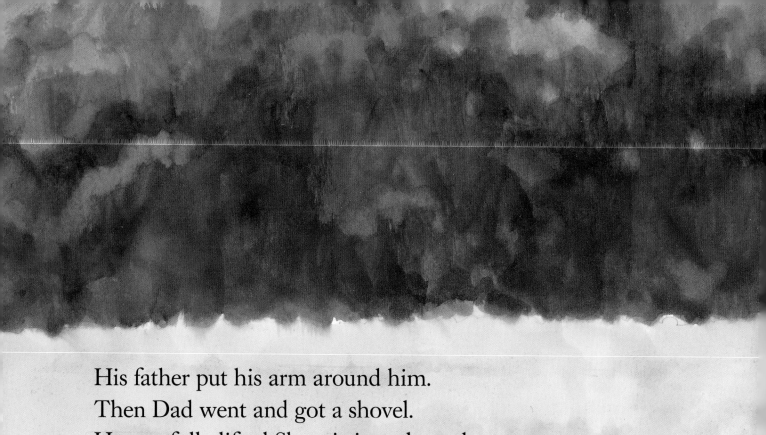

His father put his arm around him.
Then Dad went and got a shovel.
He carefully lifted Sheepie into the red wagon.
He pulled the wagon through the pasture toward the river.
Behind them, the sun was starting to go down.

When they got to the river, Dad took the shovel
and began to dig in the soft dirt.
"Will Sheepie ever come back?" Owen asked.
His father stopped digging.
"No," he said. "But he'll stay with us, in a way.
He'll become part of our happy memories."

"Remember playing at the lake? And remember
how he held up one paw to shake your hand?
No matter how far you tossed the ball,
he dog-paddled out and brought it back.
Sheepie was a good dog," said Dad.

The shovel went *swoosh* in the dirt.
Owen listened to his father's deep breathing.
The hole got deeper and wider.

Dad took the blanket and wrapped it around Sheepie.

"Wait," said Owen. "I want to pet Sheepie one more time."
He touched Sheepie's face and furry neck.
"Daddy, I can't play with Sheepie anymore."
Owen felt tears well up, and he looked away.

"I know," said his father. "It's not easy.
You two were pals, real pals."

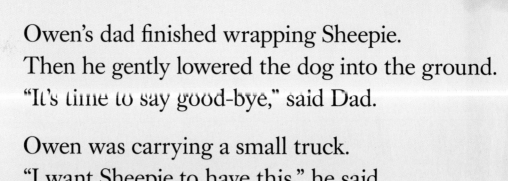

Owen's dad finished wrapping Sheepie.
Then he gently lowered the dog into the ground.
"It's time to say good-bye," said Dad.

Owen was carrying a small truck.
"I want Sheepie to have this," he said.

Owen put the little truck carefully beside Sheepie.
Then his dad filled the hole with dirt.

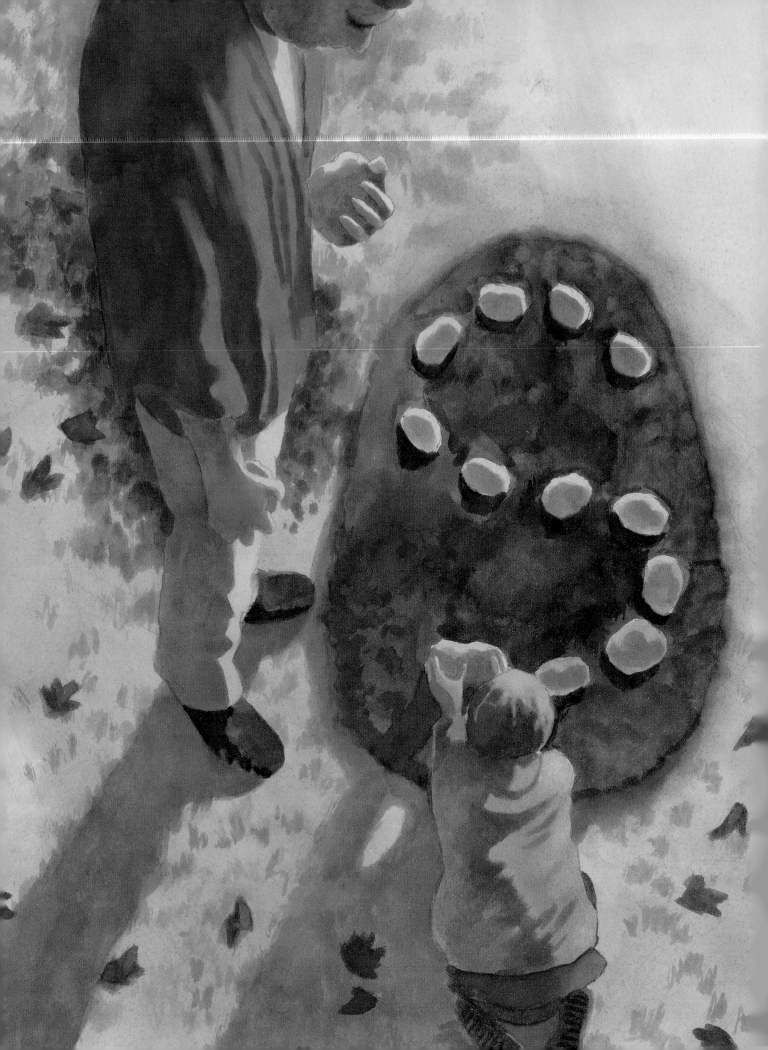

"We should look for some stones," said Dad.
Together they gathered stones from the river's edge.
The water was cool. And the wet stones were shiny.
They placed them on top of the grave in the shape
of a big, curvy *S*.

"We can come visit whenever we want to," said Dad.

The sky was turning darker. It was time to go.
Owen climbed into the wagon, and Dad pulled him home.

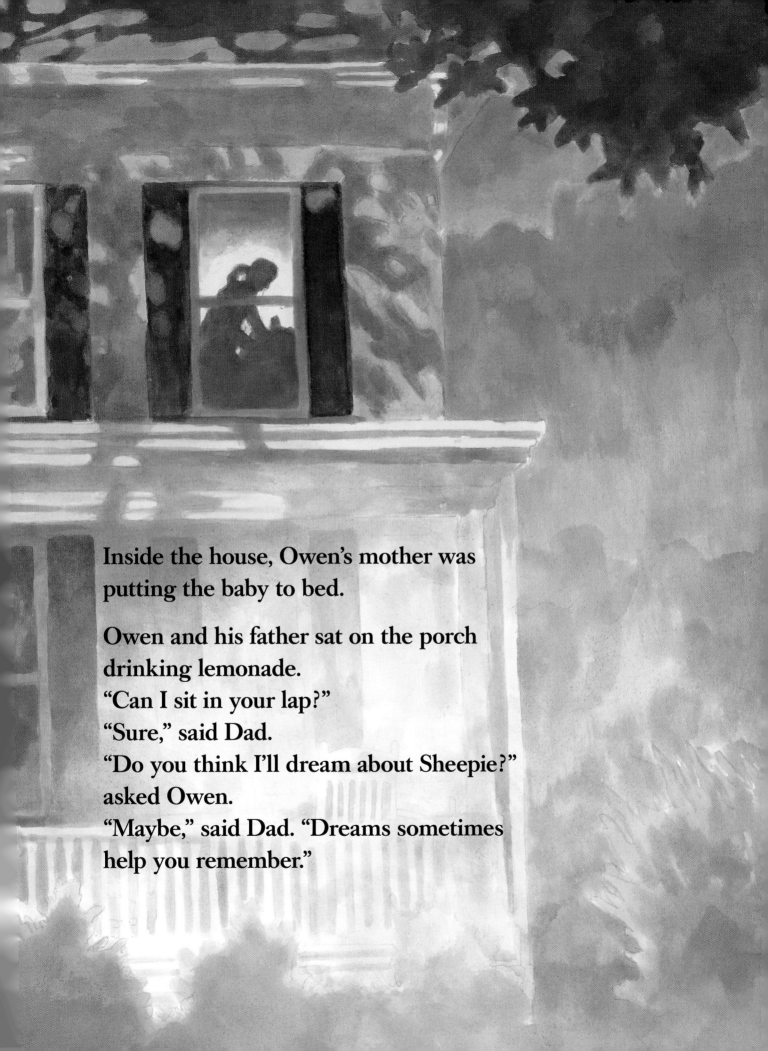

Inside the house, Owen's mother was putting the baby to bed.

Owen and his father sat on the porch drinking lemonade.
"Can I sit in your lap?"
"Sure," said Dad.
"Do you think I'll dream about Sheepie?" asked Owen.
"Maybe," said Dad. "Dreams sometimes help you remember."

Owen felt warm with his father's
arms around him.
His eyelids fluttered.
The moon rose above the trees.
Then Owen whispered softly,
"Good-bye, Sheepie. Good-bye."